Ready, Aim, Whoops!

Joe waited for Zack to stand up to throw a snowball. Joe raised his arm and threw with all his might. Zack ducked, and the snowball hit Danny Otley full in the face.

"Ow! Ooowww!" Danny started yelling. "That hurt! I'm telling my big brother on you, Joe Hardy!" he yelled. "You're going to be sorry!"

Danny ran to a big black pickup truck. A mean-looking teenage boy got out. Joe and Frank watched Danny talking to him and then pointing at them. The mean-looking boy started to walk in their direction.

Frank looked at Joe. "I think we're in big trouble," he muttered.

The Hardy Boys® are The Clues Brothers™

Available from MINSTREL Books

The Hardy Boys® are:

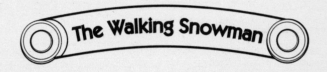

THE CLUES BROTHERS.™ 10

The Walking Snowman

Franklin W. Dixon

**Illustrated by
Marcy Ramsey**

A
MINSTREL®
BOOK

Published by POCKET BOOKS
New York   London   Toronto   Sydney   Tokyo   Singapore

This book is a work of fiction. Names, characters, places, and incidents are products of the author's imagination or are used fictitiously. Any resemblance to actual events or locales or persons living or dead is entirely coincidental.

A MINSTREL PAPERBACK *Original*

A Minstrel Book published by
POCKET BOOKS, a division of Simon & Schuster Inc.
1230 Avenue of the Americas, New York, NY 10020

Copyright © 1999 by Simon & Schuster Inc.

Front cover illustration by Thompson Studio

ISBN: 0-671-02560-0

First Minstrel Books paperback printing January 1999

10 9 8 7 6 5 4 3 2

THE HARDY BOYS® ARE THE CLUES BROTHERS is a trademark of Simon & Schuster Inc.

THE HARDY BOYS, A MINSTREL BOOK and colophon are registered trademarks of Simon & Schuster Inc.

Printed in the U.S.A.

QBP/✕

1

Cheater Joe

It's snowing!" eight-year-old Joe Hardy yelled. He was walking to school with his nine-year-old brother, Frank. "Look, a snowflake just landed on my sleeve. It really does have six points!"

Frank looked up at the sky. It was heavy with yellowish gray clouds. "And a lot more snowflakes are about to join it," he said. "The weatherman on TV said that a big snowstorm was headed our way."

"Cool!" Joe said. "I love snow, don't you? Winter is my favorite time of year."

"You said summer was your favorite time of year when we went camping," Frank reminded him. "And you said fall was your favorite time when we got to play in the leaves."

"So, winter's my favorite time now," Joe said firmly. "It's not fair we have to go to school the first day it snows. We should have a First Snowy Day holiday."

"I'm all for extra holidays," Frank said, "but there isn't even enough snow to make snowballs yet. It needs to keep on snowing all day. Then it will be awesome by this afternoon when school gets out."

"Hey, wait up, you guys," a voice called behind them. They looked around. Their friend Chet Morton was running to meet them—though he was waddling rather than running. He was wearing so many layers of clothes that he found it hard to move.

"My mom made me wear all this stuff," he gasped. "I can hardly move. And you know the worst thing? I can't lift my arm to my mouth. I'm having a major snack attack.

I'll die of hunger before we reach school."

Frank and Joe laughed.

"You're always hungry, Chet," Frank said.

"What are you doing?" Chet asked Joe suddenly.

Joe was walking with his tongue sticking out.

"Eating snowflakes," Joe said. "Mmm. They taste good."

Frank shook his head. "You're weird, sometimes."

Chet stuck his tongue out, too. "They don't taste nearly as good as chips." Chet sounded disappointed. "In fact they only taste of . . . snow."

They stomped on. It was snowing harder now. A coat of snowflakes was sticking to the fronts of their jackets.

"I wish I hadn't tried eating snow," Chet said. "Now I'm really hungry, and my chips are inside my jacket where I can't reach them."

"It's okay, Chet. We're nearly there," Joe said. He pointed at the school entrance ahead of them.

The school yard was full of excited kids rushing out of school buses into the snow. Before they could think of playing in the snow, the bell rang.

"Yo, Hardy. Snowball fight at recess," a boy in Frank's fourth-grade class yelled.

Joe wondered if the fourth-graders would let him join the snowball fight. He loved snowball fights, even if he did seem to end up with snow down his neck. He looked around for his friends in Mrs. Adair's third-grade class. Maybe they'd have their own snowball fight at recess. Or better still—maybe they'd get together and build the world's biggest snowman!

As Joe came into the classroom, he saw that all the kids were gathered around Danny Otley.

"They cost almost a hundred dollars," Danny was saying. He was holding up his foot. Joe could see he was wearing a new white-and-purple basketball shoe.

"Wow! Skyjumpers!" Some of the kids sounded really impressed.

4

Joe pretended not to be interested. He didn't like Danny Otley. He was a show-off and a troublemaker, too. Worse still, he now sat next to Joe. Mrs. Adair had moved the seats around after winter break. Joe would rather sit next to a girl than Danny Otley. He was always whispering and asking Joe the answer and getting Joe in trouble.

"See my new Skyjumpers, Joe?" Danny said as Mrs. Adair made them take their seats. "I bet you wish you could have a pair, don't you? My big brother bought them for me."

Secretly Joe wished that he could have a pair of the famous new basketball shoes, but he wasn't going to tell that to Danny.

"They're okay," he said, and got out his books.

All morning long it snowed and snowed. When Joe looked out the window, all he could see was swirling whiteness. No cars, no trees, no fence—just snow. Now there would definitely be enough to make a snowman.

"You want to make a snowman at recess?" he asked his friend Mike Mendez.

"Cool," Mike said.

"Yeah, really cool—freezing, in fact." Joe laughed.

"I'm not making a snowman. I'd get my new shoes wet, and they cost a hundred dollars," Danny said.

Joe and Mike exchanged grins. They were both glad that Danny didn't want to make a snowman with them.

But when it was time for recess, Ms. Vaughn, the principal, came on the intercom. "Boys and girls, it's snowing too hard. Everyone is to stay in their classrooms today," she said.

Joe groaned and looked across at Mike. "That's not fair," he said. "We won't get to make our snowman."

"It's snowing pretty hard out there," Mike said. "We might not find our way back to the classroom again."

"Then we'd get to skip the math test," Joe said with a laugh.

"I wonder if we'll be snowed in," Katie Hansen said worriedly. "We might get stuck here."

"Yeah, we might be snowed in for weeks. We'd run out of food and have to start eating each other," Tony Prito said.

"Eeuwww, gross," Katie said.

The boys laughed.

"Maybe Mrs. Vaughn will let us go home early," Joe suggested. "Wouldn't that be great?"

"Yeah, right." Mike made a face. "How often do they let us out early?"

"Wouldn't it be great if there was a trick in my magic book to make clocks go faster?" Joe said. He had taken a magic book out of the library. He and Frank had a magic set at home.

Mike's face lit up. "Maybe that's a new invention I could work on—a remote control for a clock. Interesting."

He was deep in thought as he walked

back to his seat. Mike loved to invent things.

The day seemed to drag on and on. By afternoon it was hot and stuffy in the classroom. The kids found it hard to stay awake.

"Time for our math test," Mrs. Adair said. "That will wake you all up. Twenty questions in thirty minutes." She passed out papers, then she said, "Ready. Go."

Joe started doing the math problems. He was good at math. He worked his way quickly down the page. When he was almost done, he looked up to see how much time was left. He still had fifteen minutes. He glanced out the window to see if it was still snowing hard.

Then Danny Otley raised his hand. "Please, Mrs. Adair. Joe Hardy is cheating," he said.

2

Ready, Aim, Whoops!

Joe's face turned very red.

"I am not cheating!" he said angrily.

"Joe was looking at my answers. I saw him," Danny said.

"I did see you looking in Danny's direction, Joe." Mrs. Adair frowned. She didn't want to believe that Joe was cheating.

"I've almost finished my test," Joe said, holding up the paper. "Why would I need to copy Danny's answers? I just wanted to see if it was still snowing hard."

Mrs. Adair nodded. "Please keep your

eyes on your own work from now on, Joe."
Then she smiled. "Although I must admit
that the snow does look tempting, doesn't
it?"

Joe thought Mrs. Adair was the nicest
teacher in the world. He finished his test
and brought his paper to the front desk. On
the way back he made a face at Danny Otley.

"Tattletale," he whispered.

"When you have finished your math you
may read your library books," Mrs. Adair
said.

Joe opened the magic book he had taken
from the library. Wouldn't it be neat if
magic tricks really worked, Joe thought. He
wished he had a real magic wand, not just a
fake like the one in their magic set at home.
Then he'd wave it at the clock and poof—
school would be over. He closed his eyes
and pretended to wave a magic wand at the
clock.

At that moment Ms. Vaughn's voice came
on the intercom again. "Listen up, boys and
girls. I am sending everyone home fifteen

minutes early today. It's not snowing right now. I want you to get home safely before it starts again."

Joe grinned at his friend Mike. "How was that, Mike? I waved my magic wand at the clock."

Danny Otley overheard. "Are you still into that dumb magic stuff?" he sneered.

"Get lost, Otley," Joe said. "At least I got us out of class early."

"I'll have to call my brother to have him come and pick me up early," Danny said. "He's got a cell phone in his truck."

"That guy is a pain," Mike muttered. He walked with Joe out of the classroom.

"Tell me about it," Joe said. "I wish he didn't sit next to me."

He put on his jacket and gloves and ran out into the snow. He stood looking for his brother. Suddenly a snowball hit him hard in the back.

Joe spun around.

"Gotcha, Joe," Frank said, grinning. "Get over here."

He was crouching with some other fourth graders behind a big pile of backpacks. A snowball came flying and hit Joe's arm. Across the school yard was another pile of backpacks with more fourth graders behind it. Snowballs were whizzing through the air. Joe ran over to Frank and started making his own snowballs.

Chet was coming toward them. Frank threw a snowball at him. It hit Chet full in the chest.

"Ow," Chet yelled. "What did you have to go and do that for?" He looked really upset.

"Come on, Chet," Frank called. "I didn't really hurt you. You're wearing too many clothes."

"You didn't hurt me," Chet said, "but you might have squashed my last bag of chips. They were in my top pocket."

He wriggled around until he drew out the bag of chips. A big smile spread across his face. "It's okay. They're not squashed. See you guys."

He walked away, happily eating.

Just then a very hard snowball hit Joe on the head. It really stung.

He looked around to see Zack Jackson, the meanest guy in school, laughing at him. He had sneaked up behind them.

"Gotcha, Hardy," he yelled.

"Just you wait," Joe yelled back. He stooped to scoop up a handful of snow.

"Ooh, I am so scared," Zack jeered. "Betcha miss me. You've got the wimpiest arm in the school."

"Have not!" Joe yelled. He was really mad now. He packed his snowball down until it was big and hard, just like Zack's.

"I'm going to get Zack," he said to Frank. "This is a super-deluxe snowball."

"Great," Frank said. "Go for it."

Joe waited for Zack to stand up to throw a snowball. Joe raised his arm and threw with all his might. Zack saw the snowball coming and ducked. The snowball whizzed over his head. Danny Otley was right behind him. The snowball hit him full in the face.

"Ow! Ooowwww!" Danny Otley started yelling. "That hurt." He brushed away the snow and saw Joe standing there. "I'm telling my big brother on you, Joe Hardy," he yelled. "You're going to be sorry!"

He ran to a big black pickup truck that was parked at the curb. A mean-looking teenage boy got out. He was wearing tight black jeans and a big red sweater with a down vest over it. Joe and Frank watched Danny talking to him and then pointing at them. The mean-looking boy started to walk in their direction.

Frank looked at Joe. "I think we're in big trouble," he muttered.

3

A Totally Awesome Snowman

Before Danny Otley and his mean brother reached the Hardys, Ms. Vaughn came out. She clapped her hands. "Everyone, go home right now," she said. "I let you out early so that you could get home before it snows again. Go on, off you go."

She stood there, watching. Frank and Joe didn't wait to be told twice. They picked up their backpacks and headed out of the school yard, past Danny and his brother.

"You'll be sorry," Danny yelled after them.

Frank looked around when they got to the end of the street. "Whew! They're not following us," he said.

"Danny Otley's brother looked mean, didn't he?" Joe said to Frank as they hurried home. "But that figures. Danny is mean, too."

"Forget about it," Frank said. "They're not going to spoil our fun."

Joe nodded. "Let's build a snowman before it snows again," he said as they reached their house.

"Whoa! Hold it right there," Mrs. Hardy called as Frank and Joe opened the front door. "Don't come in. You're covered in snow. You look like walking snowmen."

"It's okay, Mom. We don't want to come in," Joe said. "We want to build a snowman before it gets dark."

"I'd like you to do me a favor first," Mrs. Hardy said. "Mrs. Hammel had someone clear her front path today, but it's been snowing again. I think it would be nice if you boys made sure her front path was free of snow."

"Sure. We can do that," Frank said. "It won't take us long."

They got shovels from the garage and scraped away the snow from Mrs. Hammel's front path. The path wasn't very long, but using the big shovels was hard work.

"I'm pooped," Joe gasped. "I don't think I have enough energy to make a snowman now."

Just as they were finishing up, the front door opened, and Mrs. Hammel looked out. She was a little old lady, not much taller than Frank. She had wispy white hair around her wrinkled face.

"What kind boys you are," she said. "I thought I'd have to call the man to clear my path again. I don't like to go out in the snow—I'm really scared of falling. Please come inside. I've just baked cookies, and I'll make you some hot chocolate."

Frank looked at Joe. "I guess the snowman could wait a little while longer," he said.

"You bet," Joe said. "I'm starving after that hard work. And your cookies are the best, Mrs. Hammel."

The boys took off their boots before they went into Mrs. Hammel's warm kitchen. She put a plate of cookies on the table. "Help yourselves," she said.

Frank and Joe each took a big, warm cookie.

"Delicious, Mrs. Hammel," Joe said.

Mrs. Hammel smiled. "You're lucky. I don't often bake anymore. There's no point when it's just me and Princess, and she doesn't like cookies."

She stroked the white cat that was curled up on a chair. "I'd be very lonely if it wasn't for her," Mrs. Hammel said. "And for kind boys like you."

The kettle boiled, and she put two mugs of steaming hot chocolate in front of them. Then she sat with Princess on her knee.

As soon as they had finished their snack, Frank and Joe got up and thanked Mrs. Hammel.

"We have to go now," Frank said. "We want to build a snowman before it gets dark."

"Come back soon," Mrs. Hammel said.

"She's a nice lady," Joe whispered as they put their boots on again. "And she bakes good cookies. Now I'm full of energy and ready to build the world's biggest snowman."

There was deep, new snow all over their front yard. Frank and Joe started rolling a ball. They made it bigger and bigger until it was hard to push.

"Let's start a second ball now," Frank suggested.

They rolled a second ball of snow until that was almost as big as the first.

"Wait a second!" Joe cried. "How are we going to get this ball of snow on top of the other one? It's huge. We'll never lift it."

"I've got an idea," Frank said. "Stay there. I'll be right back."

He ran into the garage and came back with a plank of wood.

"What are we going to do with that—build a house for the snowman?" Joe asked.

"No, dummy." Frank laughed. "In social studies we read about the Egyptians. They used ramps to make the pyramids. They dragged big blocks of stone up ramps. We can make a ramp for our snowman."

"Wow," Joe said. "Sometimes you're pretty smart, Frank."

"Lucky one Hardy brother has brains, huh?" Frank said with a grin.

They leaned the board on top of the bigger snowball. Then they rolled the second snowball slowly up until it was at the top. Then they carefully moved the plank away.

"It worked!" Joe yelled excitedly. "Now all we need is a head."

They made a third ball of snow and stood on tiptoe to put it on top.

"This is a really awesome snowman." Frank sounded pleased. "Now we need to dress him."

They opened the front door.

"Mom, come and see our snowman," Frank called.

Mrs. Hardy looked out the window. "That's a very big snowman, boys," she said.

"We need to finish it," Joe said. "Can we come inside and get stuff?"

"What do you need?" Mrs. Hardy asked. "I'll bring it out to you."

"A carrot for his nose," Joe said.

"And buttons for eyes," Frank added. "And something for his mouth?"

"Chocolate-covered peanuts," Joe suggested. "We have some, don't we?"

Soon the snowman had a face.

"Now we need to dress him," Frank said.

"You can look in that bag of old clothes," Mrs. Hardy said. "I'm sending it to the thrift store. Help yourselves."

Frank and Joe tipped out the clothes.

"Look, here's Dad's old fishing hat!" Joe exclaimed.

"And a scarf and big old gardening gloves," Frank added.

They put the clothes on the snowman. They filled the gloves with snow and gave the man snow arms, too. He began to look very real.

"If he's a fisherman, he needs a rod," Frank suggested. "There's that old broken rod in the shed."

Soon the snowman had a rod. Then they made a big fish out of snow and put it next to the snowman.

"Now he's perfect!" Joe exclaimed. "Mom, come and see our snow fisherman!"

At that moment the boys' father drove up. He worked as a detective and had his own agency in Bayport. He pulled into the garage and got out of his car.

"What a lot of snow," he said. "It was really hard driving home." He started to walk toward the house when he noticed the snowman. "Did you boys build that?" he asked.

Frank and Joe nodded.

"That is one fine snowman," Mr. Hardy said. "It's too bad you built it here, because there's going to be a snowman contest in the park tomorrow."

"Really?" Joe asked excitedly. "We could enter our snowman."

"Joe, we could never move that snowman," Frank said. "It's way too big. We'll just have to build another snowman for the contest tomorrow. At least we've had practice now."

"Is that my old fishing hat?" Mr. Hardy asked. "I wondered where that had gotten to."

"Mom was going to throw it out," Joe said.

"I bought you a new one, Fenton," Mrs. Hardy said, coming out to join them.

"Yes, but I like the old one better," Mr. Hardy said.

"Fenton, it's falling to pieces." Mrs. Hardy laughed.

"But it's my lucky hat," Mr. Hardy said firmly. "Thanks for rescuing it for me, boys."

They went in to eat dinner.

Later Joe looked out his bedroom window. Moonlight was shining on the snowman.

"He looks almost real," Joe said to Frank. "Wouldn't it be neat if our magic wand could bring him to life?"

"Joe, magic tricks are only tricks," Frank said. "But he does look almost real, doesn't he?"

"He's the best snowman we've ever built," Joe said proudly.

That night Joe dreamed of winning the snowman contest. But when the judge went to pin the blue ribbon on the snowman, it came to life and walked away.

When he opened his eyes, the sun was shining. He jumped out of bed and ran to the window. There was the snowy front lawn, but it was empty. Joe stared, blinked his eyes, then stared again.

"Frank!" he yelled. "Get in here right now. Our snowman has vanished!"

4

The Mysterious Footprints

Frank opened a sleepy eye and saw Joe standing beside his bed. "Whassamatter?" he asked. "Go back to sleep. It's Saturday. We don't need to get up early."

"Our snowman's gone!" Joe exclaimed.

"Ha ha. Very funny," Frank said, pulling the covers over his head.

"No, I'm serious," Joe said. "I looked out of my window and it's not there, Frank. Our snowman is missing."

Frank jumped out of bed and ran into Joe's room. He looked out of Joe's window. His eyes opened very wide in surprise.

"I don't believe it!" he said. "It really has gone. Let's check it out."

The boys pulled on sweats and socks over their pj's. They ran downstairs and put on their boots and jackets. Then they ran outside into the crisp snow.

They could see where the snowman had been. They could see their footprints where they had made the snowman. The plank of wood was lying close to where the snowman had been. But there was no sign of the snowman.

"That's really weird," Frank said, staring at the snowy ground. "If someone smashed our snowman there would be a big pile of snow lying around. But there's no extra snow here."

"Someone must have taken our snowman," Joe said.

Frank shook his head. "How could someone take him? He was too heavy for us to move him."

"And I see something else weird," Joe said. "Look at the footprints. Here are all the prints we made when we built the snowman. Our prints go to the house and to the garage. But there are no prints at all leading from the snowman to the street."

"You're right, Joe," Frank said. "How could anyone have taken our snowman without making any footprints?"

"Maybe our snowman came to life and walked away," Joe said with a grin.

"You're too much into this magic stuff, Joe," Frank said. "Snowmen don't come to life."

"Then how do you explain this?" Joe asked. His voice was shaking with excitement. He pointed at the ground near the snowman. There was a huge, round footprint.

"Here's another, and another," Frank said. The trail of big round prints crossed their yard and went on down the street.

"Now do you believe me?" Joe demanded. "The snowman came to life and

walked away. What else could have made those footprints?"

"That's what we're going to find out," Frank said. "Let's follow the footprints, Joe. Maybe they'll lead us to the person who took our snowman."

They set off down the street. The footprints crossed several yards. They went around trees and bushes. They even went up someone's front steps and then down again.

"This is a crazy trail, Joe," Frank said. "What was the person doing?"

"I told you, it wasn't a person, it was our snowman," Joe said. "He had big round feet."

"Get real, Joe. Snowmen can't walk," Frank said. "Something else had to have made these prints."

"Like what?"

Frank shrugged. "I have no idea. I've never seen anything like it."

"I think the snowman wanted to check out the neighborhood," Joe insisted.

They tracked the footprints almost to the end of their street. The corner house had a big yard with lots of bushes in it.

"Look, the tracks go into this yard," Frank said. The round tracks went across the snowy lawn and in and out of the bushes.

Suddenly Joe grabbed Frank. "Look!" he whispered.

Frank turned to look where Joe was pointing. He was just in time to see a round white figure go behind a clump of bushes.

The boys crept closer. They could hear heavy breathing on the other side of a big bush. Carefully they parted the branches and peeked through.

Then they gasped and jumped back. On the other side of the bush, only a few inches away from them, eyes were staring back at them.

5

The Missing Princess

The boys gasped and jumped back. At the same moment, they heard a sound on the other side of the bush. It was a very human gasp, and then a voice said, "Oh, my. Oh, deary me."

"I know that voice," Frank said. "It's Mrs. Hammel."

They rushed around the hedge and found Mrs. Hammel standing there, bundled in a white furry coat.

"Oh, boys, you scared me," she said.

"Sorry, Mrs. Hammel," Frank answered.

He didn't like to say that she had scared them, too. "What are you doing out in all this snow? You said you didn't like to go out in the snow anymore."

"You're right, I hate to go out in the snow," Mrs. Hammel said. "I'm scared of slipping and falling. But it's an emergency. I had to go out."

Joe had just noticed Mrs. Hammel's feet.

"Look, Frank." He dug his brother in the side. "Now we know who made the big round footprints. It wasn't the snowman. It was Mrs. Hammel."

The boys stared at Mrs. Hammel's feet. They couldn't see her shoes, because she had pieces of old blanket tied around her feet.

"Mrs. Hammel, what do you have on your feet?" Joe asked.

"I told you I was scared of slipping on icy patches," Mrs. Hammel said. "That's why I wrapped these pieces of old blanket over my shoes. That's what we used to do in icy weather when I was a girl, back in

Minnesota. It works well." She looked at the ground. "It makes funny footprints, doesn't it?"

"It sure does," Frank said, giving Joe a look. "We've been following your footprints all the way down our street. Why have you been wandering through all the yards?"

"Princess is missing," Mrs. Hammel said. "I've been looking everywhere for her."

"Princess is missing? That's terrible," Joe said. "How did she get out?"

"It must have been early this morning when I went to get the newspaper," Mrs. Hammel said. "I always keep her inside during bad weather. I left the door open for only a minute or two while I walked down the front path to get the paper. She must have slipped out then. I called and called, but she's nowhere to be found. I hope nothing has happened to her."

"We'll help you find her, Mrs. Hammel," Frank said. "Won't we, Joe?"

"Oh . . . sure," Joe said. He tried to sound

cheerful, but he wanted to solve the mystery of their missing snowman.

"It won't be easy," Mrs. Hammel said. "Princess is pure white. She'll be hard to see in the snow."

"She must have left prints," Frank said. "Look how we followed your footprints to find you. Let's go back to your house and look for her footprints in the snow."

"What a smart boy you are," Mrs. Hammel said.

"Our dad's a detective," Joe said. "We're learning to be good detectives, too. He's teaching us how to follow clues."

Mrs. Hammel looked happier as she walked back down the street with Joe and Frank.

"Okay," Frank said. "Let's start close to your front door."

"Here are some prints," Joe called. "An animal went this way."

They followed neat little prints across the snowy lawn.

"They lead to this big tree," Joe said.

"That's it," Mrs. Hammel said. "Princess climbed the tree because she didn't like the feel of snow on her paws."

The boys stood under the tree and looked up.

"I don't see any white cat up there," Frank said. "Give me a hand, Joe. I'll see if I can climb up."

Frank managed to pull himself up as far as the first branch. A squirrel scampered down a higher branch and made angry chittering noises at him.

Frank climbed down again. "That's what made those tracks, Mrs. Hammel. It was a squirrel."

Mrs. Hammel smiled. "I know that squirrel. He comes to take the seed I put out for the birds."

"Let's see if there are any more tracks, Frank," Joe said.

They searched the front yard.

"Here we are. These tracks cross the front yard and go on down the street," Frank said. "Come on, Joe. Let's follow them."

Joe and Frank ran down the street, following the paw prints.

"I hope we find Princess this time," Frank said. "Poor Mrs. Hammel is very upset."

"And I want to get back to finding our snowman," Joe added. "And my stomach says it's breakfast time, too."

They reached the end of the street. The paw prints turned right. Joe and Frank followed.

"They go up this front path," Joe said. "All the way to the front door. Maybe Princess was kidnapped by the people who live here."

"We can't knock on their door and ask if they've stolen a cat," Frank said.

"We can ask if they've *seen* a white cat," Joe suggested.

Frank rang the doorbell. There was the sound of loud barking. A man came to the door, and immediately a brown-and-white dog pushed past him, barking at the boys.

"Quiet, Sumo," the man said, grabbing the dog's collar. "What do you boys want?"

"We're looking for a missing white cat," Frank said.

The man laughed. "Well, it isn't here. Sumo would chase it and try to eat it. Calm down, Sumo," he added as the dog tried to jump up at the boys. "He's got too much energy. And I've just given him a long walk, too."

"All the way down Elm Street?" Joe asked.

"That's right," the man said.

"Thank you anyway," the boys said.

Frank looked at Joe as they made their way back to Mrs. Hammel's house. Joe shrugged. "How were we to know they were dog tracks and not cat tracks?" he asked.

"I've been thinking," Frank said. "Don't cats keep their claws tucked away? See how those prints were pointed where the claws stuck out? We need to look for prints with no claws."

They searched around Mrs. Hammel's house, but they couldn't find any more prints at all.

"I don't get it," Joe said. "It stopped snowing yesterday evening. If Princess went out this morning, we'd see her footprints in the snow."

"You know what this means, don't you?" Frank asked excitedly. "It means that Princess never went out at all!"

6

One Case Solved, One to Go

The Hardy brothers ran up to Mrs. Hammel's front door and knocked.

"May we help you look for Princess inside your house?" Frank asked. "We don't think she went out. That means she's still here."

"But I looked everywhere," Mrs. Hammel said. "And I called and called."

"Maybe she got shut in a closet," Joe suggested.

"You're welcome to search again," Mrs. Hammel said, "but I can't think where she could be."

They searched from room to room, but

there was no sign of Princess. At last the boys found a door under the stairs.

"Where does this lead, Mrs. Hammel?" Frank asked.

"Only to the basement," she said.

She opened the door and turned on a light switch. The dim light shone on a flight of stairs going down.

"She wouldn't be down here," Mrs. Hammel said. "I hardly ever go down here—there's only the furnace and the washing machine and dryer."

Joe peeked down the dark stairway.

"Did you go down today, Mrs. Hammel?" he asked.

"Just to put some laundry in the laundry basket."

"Maybe we should check it out then," Frank said.

"Watch your step," Mrs. Hammel said. "The light is bad. It's hard to see well."

"You go first," Joe said to Frank.

"Thanks a lot," Frank said. He went carefully down the steep stairs.

"I don't see why a cat would want to be down here," Frank turned to Joe. "There are no soft chairs or pillows."

The boys looked behind the stack of old magazines. They looked under an old chest of drawers. Joe peeked into the laundry basket. Then he laughed. "Some laundry and one white cat, Mrs. Hammel."

Princess was fast asleep among the white sheets.

Mrs. Hammel came down the stairs. "Well, imagine that," she said, starting to laugh, too. "My eyesight's not too good anymore. I didn't see her because she's white and the sheets are white." She picked up Princess and smiled at the boys. "Thank you for finding her."

They started back up the stairs. "I hope you'll stay and have some more of my cookies and hot chocolate as a reward, boys," Mrs. Hammel said.

"Thanks, Mrs. Hammel, but we've got another mystery to solve," Joe said. "You didn't see a snowman when you were out looking for Princess, did you?"

"A snowman?" Mrs. Hammel shook her head.

"Let's get back to work, Joe," Frank said. "I'm glad we found Princess. I get the feeling that the snowman mystery isn't going to be so easy to solve."

As they went back to their own front yard Frank stopped and pointed at the ground.

"Look, Joe. I didn't notice this before. What do you think it is?"

A trail of bright orange crumbs went up to their front door. Then the trail turned around and went away again.

"I don't know what it is," Joe said, "but maybe it has something to do with our missing snowman. Let's follow it."

They ran back down the street, following the orange trail until they caught up with Chet.

"Hey, guys, want a cheese puff?" he called when he saw them.

He held out an almost empty bag. His fingers were orange.

"What were you doing at our house, Chet?"

"How did you know I was just at your house?"

"We're the Clues Brothers. We're detectives," Joe said. "You left a trail of clues behind you—orange crumbs."

"Oh, that," Chet said. "I came to see if you guys wanted to enter the snowman contest in the park."

"We wanted to," Joe said, "but we're trying to solve a mystery. The snowman we made last night disappeared from our front yard."

"How could a snowman disappear?" Chet grinned. "Are you putting me on?"

"No, really," Joe said. "We built a snowman last night. This morning it's not there."

"Maybe it went to enter itself in the contest." Chet was still grinning.

"Let's go to the park, Frank," Joe said, tugging at Frank's arm. "We're missing out on the contest. It might take us all day to solve this mystery."

"Okay," Frank said. "But first we should ask Mom and Dad if we can go to the park."

They went back to their house.

"Here you are," Mrs. Hardy said as they came in. "We wondered where you had gone. Breakfast is all ready—blueberry pancakes."

"I think you guys should definitely stop to have breakfast first," Chet said. He looked hopefully at the stack of pancakes on the griddle.

"Okay, but it has to be quick," Frank said. "We've got a busy morning ahead of us."

Mr. Hardy handed plates of pancakes to the boys. "Are you going to enter the snowman contest?" he asked.

"If it's okay to go to the park by ourselves," Frank said.

"It's fine," Mr. Hardy replied. "You don't have to cross any busy streets. Just stay together and look out for one another. Are

you going to build another snow fisherman?"

"A snow fisherman?" Chet asked, looking
up from his pancakes. "That's really weird."

"What is?" Frank and Joe asked at the
same time.

"When I came past the park the contest
had already started. One snowman was finished. He was dressed like a fisherman. He
even had a snow fish and a rod."

Frank looked at Joe. Joe looked at Frank.

"Our snowman!" they said at the same
moment.

"What are you talking about?" Chet
asked.

"That was our snowman. We built it last
night," Frank said.

"In the park?" Chet asked.

"No, in our front yard. This morning it
was gone. Someone stole it."

"Someone stole your snowman?" Mr.
Hardy asked.

"How can anyone steal a snowman?"
Chet added.

"We don't know, but we're going to find out," Frank said. "Come on."

They jumped up from the table.

"Mom, we'll have to finish breakfast later," Joe said. "We have to get to the park to find out who stole our snowman. Okay?"

Mrs. Hardy only smiled and shook her head as they struggled back into their jackets.

The boys ran all the way. By the time they got there, Chet was huffing and puffing under all his layers of clothes.

The park was full of kids building snowmen.

"Where was the snow fisherman, Chet?" Frank asked.

"Right under that big sign that says Snowman Contest, Ten-and-Under Division," Chet said.

"Look, there's our snowman!" Frank yelled.

"And look who's standing beside it!" Joe exclaimed. "Danny Otley!"

Danny Otley was standing beside the snowman, looking very proud of himself.

"You took our snowman!" Joe yelled.

Danny Otley looked worried for a moment. Then he grinned. "Prove it," he said.

"Don't worry, we'll prove it," Frank said angrily.

"You'd better stay away from me. I'll get my big brother," Danny Otley said, looking around nervously.

A man with a badge saying Contest Official stepped between the boys. "No fighting, boys," he said firmly.

"But he took our snowman," Frank said.

The man smiled. "He took your snowman? You mean he borrowed your idea?"

"No, he actually took our snowman. We built it in our front yard, and now it's missing."

A crowd had gathered around them. Kids started laughing.

"Don't be dumb. How could anyone take a snowman?" someone asked.

"I can prove it," Frank said suddenly. "The snowman is wearing our father's fishing hat." He stepped up and took the hat from the snowman's head. "See?" He held up the hat to the judge. "His initials are inside. FH. That stands for Fenton Hardy."

"Let me see that hat," the man said.

"Okay, so I might have borrowed the hat," Danny said. "But you can't make anyone believe that this is your snowman. How did it get here, walk?"

"You took it from our yard last night, somehow," Joe yelled.

Most of the other kids were laughing now.

"How, in my pockets?" Danny asked. He turned to the crowd. They laughed louder. "Besides, I don't even know where you live."

Danny looked up as three big boys pushed through the crowd. Two of them were wearing big parkas. The other one was wearing a down vest over a red sweater. They all looked mean.

"Danny's big brother," Joe muttered.

"What's happening here?" Danny's brother asked.

"Danny stole our snowman, and I bet he had you help him," Frank said.

"I think we need to sort this out," the man said. "I'm going to get one of the judges."

He disappeared into the crowd. Danny's big brother came up to Frank and Joe. "You're just jealous because this snowman is going to win," he said. "Now beat it. Get lost and don't come back."

"We'll be back," Frank said, grabbing Joe's arm. "And we'll prove that you stole our snowman."

7

The Clues Brothers Do Their Stuff

As they walked away, Chet grabbed Frank's arm. "Sorry, you guys, but I can't walk all the way back to your house," he said. "I'm too hot in all these clothes."

"That's okay. You stay here and keep an eye on Danny Otley," Frank said. "We'll see you later."

"Show the judges your dad's hat," Chet said. "That's good proof, isn't it?"

"Only that they stole the hat, not the whole snowman," Frank said. "It's going to be hard to make anyone believe they took our snowman. I can't figure out how they did it."

"I know one thing," Joe said as they left the park. "Danny Otley was lying, and I can prove it."

"How?" Frank asked.

"Two things," Joe said. He was smiling. "Danny Otley lies a lot. When he tells a lie in school his ears turn red. His ears went red when he was talking to us."

"And the other thing?"

"He said he couldn't have taken the snowman because he doesn't know where we live. He *does* know where we live. We talked about it in class once, and he said Elm Street was ugly."

"Nice going, Joe," Frank said, slapping him on the back. "We'll catch him. We'll prove the snowman is ours."

"Do you think we should get Dad and bring him back to the park with us?" Joe asked as they got close to their house. "He saw our snowman last night. He could be a witness."

Frank shook his head. "He can only say

that last night he saw a snowman just like the one in the park. Danny can just say that he copied the idea and borrowed the hat."

"We'll never be able to prove that he took our snowman," Joe said sadly.

"Yes, we will. We're good detectives, just like Dad. We'll do all the things he'd do. We'll look for clues and try to work out how Danny and his brother got our snowman out of our yard."

"It's not going to be easy." Joe sighed. "I don't see any clues at all."

"Clue number one," Frank said. "No pile of snow. That definitely means that our snowman was taken from the yard."

He looked at the snowy ground. "But there are no footprints leading to the sidewalk," he said. "How could someone have taken our snowman but not left any footprints?"

Joe shrugged. "There are no other marks in the snow either," he said. "If anyone had dragged a sled across our yard, there would be sled tracks. It's like a spaceship landed next to the snowman, grabbed him, and took off again."

"Only I don't think that Danny Otley's big brother has a spaceship," Frank said. Then his face lit up. "Wait a second," he said. "Danny's brother does have a big pickup truck. Let's go take a look."

He ran down to the street. "Yeah, I was right!" he exclaimed. "Look. See the tire tracks? Something with wide tires backed right up to the curb."

"Tire tracks!" Joe exclaimed, punching himself on the forehead. "Why didn't we think of looking for those before?"

"I guess because there were no footprints leading from the street to the snowman," Frank said. "And the neighbor's car was parked here earlier, so the tracks were hidden. Now I've got an idea how someone might have taken the snowman away without leaving footprints."

"You do? You mean the truck came into our yard? But there are no tire tracks on our lawn."

"Of course not. The truck stayed in the street," Frank said. "If it backed up to our yard, the back part of the truck would stick out, wouldn't it?"

"Yeah," Joe said. He was beginning to understand what his brother was getting at. He tried to picture the big pickup truck, backed up to the curb. "It would come about this far into our yard, don't you think?" he asked Frank. "But that's still not where the snowman was."

"I think I've got it," Frank cried excitedly. "When the truck was backed up, some guys were sitting in the truck bed. They lowered the tailgate and jumped down."

Joe closed his eyes and tried to picture the tailgate being lowered. "They jumped down right next to our snowman!" he exclaimed. Then his face fell again. "But how did they get the snowman into the truck? It was awfully heavy, Frank. I know those guys are bigger and stronger than us, but I bet they couldn't lift those big balls of snow."

Frank's face broke into a big smile. "The same way we did," he said. "They used the board. They made a ramp. They propped it against the truck. Then they took the snowman apart, and they rolled the balls up the ramp. It would be hard work, but I bet three or four big guys could do it."

"Yeah," Joe said, giving his brother a high five. "We've solved the mystery—but how are we going to prove it?"

"Here's one piece of proof," Frank said. He pointed at the snowy ground. "Look, Joe. We left the board of wood propped against the porch, didn't we? Now it's lying close to where our snowman was. Somebody definitely moved it."

"Let's go ask Dad to see if there are fingerprints on the board," Joe said.

Frank shook his head. "They'd have been wearing gloves. It's cold."

"Too bad." Joe sighed. "We can tell our story to the judge in the park, but he'll never believe it."

"Unless . . ." Frank said. He squatted

down beside the plank. "What do you think this is, Joe?"

Joe squatted down, too. Caught on the plank was something bright red. Carefully Frank pulled it from the rough wood. "It looks like yarn," he said.

"And Danny's brother was wearing a red sweater!" Joe yelled. "This is proof, isn't it, Frank?"

"It is to me," Frank said. "But I don't know if it will be for the judges—unless we can actually see where the sweater got torn."

"We could match the tire tracks to Danny's brother's tires," Joe suggested. "Aren't all tires different?"

Frank walked over to look at the tracks. "But these are pretty new," he said. "They don't have any good worn spots or cuts on them."

"Too bad," Joe said. "We can't go back to the park unless we can definitely prove that they took the snowman."

"Talking of tire tracks gives me an idea,"

Frank said. "Let's look at the footprints again. Maybe one of those guys was wearing shoes that made a print we can identify."

"Great idea," Joe said. "Why didn't we think of that before?"

"And why did we have to walk over the prints again," Frank said. "A good detective would never do that."

"But we didn't walk over this!" Joe pointed excitedly at the snow. One of the footprints stood out very clearly. It had wavy lines across the sole. In the middle was a diamond with the initials SJ inside.

"SJ—that must stand for Skyjumper," Joe said. "And Danny was bragging about his new pair of Skyjumper shoes yesterday."

8

Danny Keeps a Cool Head

On the Hardys' way back to the park they met Chet, running to find them.

"You'd better get back to the park right now," he gasped. "They've finished judging the contest. They're starting to hand out the ribbons."

"Come on. Run," Frank yelled.

Frank and Joe sprinted down the street. Chet tried to keep up with them, puffing and panting.

"I just hope we're not too late," Frank panted as he ran.

"I'll be so mad if Danny Otley got my blue ribbon," Joe agreed.

It seemed to take forever to get to the park. The boys were hot and tired by the time they ran in through the park gates. They headed for the banner saying Snowman Contest.

Some of the snowmen in the older age groups already had blue, red, and white ribbons on them. As the boys came up they heard an announcer's voice saying, "And in the ten-and-under division, the winner is Danny Otley for his snow fisherman."

Frank and Joe pushed their way through the crowd as Chet hung back.

"Just a minute!" Frank yelled. "That blue ribbon belongs to my brother and me."

The judge paused with the blue ribbon in his hand.

"Has there been some mix-up?" he asked.

"There sure has," Joe said angrily. "Danny Otley stole the snowman that we built last night, and we can prove it."

"Not those nutty kids again," someone in the crowd growled.

"Get on with it," someone else yelled.

"We've got proof that he didn't build this snowman," Frank said, pointing at Danny.

Danny was standing beside the snowman. He glanced around nervously. "Gene?" he called. "Where are you, Gene?"

"Just a minute while I call over the head judge," the judge said. "He should hear any complaints of cheating."

A man wearing glasses and a hat came over to join them.

"Now, then, what's the problem here?" he asked, smiling at the boys.

"We built this snowman, and he took it from our yard," Frank said.

The big man went on smiling. "Took it from your yard?"

"Yes," Joe said, stepping up beside Frank. "And we know how he did it, too. His big brother backed up his truck and let down the tailgate so that it was close to our snowman. Then they took the snowman apart and rolled the biggest balls up a board into the truck."

"Interesting," the man said.

"The kid is talking nonsense," a voice said. Danny's big brother, Gene, pushed through the crowd. "I don't know how he came up with that crazy idea. He must have some terrific imagination."

"And some proof," Frank said. He reached into his pocket. "Here's what we found on the wooden board in our yard." He held up the scrap of red yarn. "I think it came from your sweater when you were moving the board last night."

"Look, Frank," Joe said. "There's a place on his sleeve where the yarn is torn."

Gene's eyes darted around the crowd. "But that still doesn't prove anything." He didn't sound too worried or scared. "How many people in Bayport wear red sweaters, huh? I could have snagged that sleeve any-where."

"We have one more piece of proof,"

Frank said. He went over to Danny. "Danny, would you please show us the shoes you're wearing?"

"What for?" Danny demanded.

"Because you're wearing brand-new Skyjumpers," Frank said. "They make a print that's very easy to spot. It has a diamond with SJ on the sole. There's a print just like that beside the place where our snowman stood."

Danny glared at his brother. "He made me do it," he said. "I didn't want to."

"Shut up, you little wimp," Gene growled. "You were the one who begged us to get even with the Hardy boys."

"Stop, I've heard enough." The head judge stepped between them, holding up his hand. "It's quite clear to me that this snowman belongs to those two young men. You took it from their yard."

He turned to Frank and Joe. "What are your names?"

"Frank and Joe Hardy, sir," Frank said.

The man cleared his throat. "I declare

that Frank and Joe Hardy have won first prize in the snowman contest," he said. He put the blue ribbon on the snow fisherman. "And here is a gift certificate to the ice cream parlor to go with it," he added.

"Thank you," Joe and Frank said together.

Danny let out a wail. "They get the certificate to the ice cream parlor? No fair!"

"And as for you, young man," the head judge said, turning to Danny, "I'd be careful if I were you. Taking other people's property can land you in a lot of trouble."

"It was a dumb snowman anyway," Danny said, scowling at Frank and Joe.

He kicked the snowman hard. "Dumb snowman!" he yelled.

The snow head wobbled and toppled onto Danny.

"Owww!" Danny yelled as the ball of snow hit him and covered him with snow.

Frank and Joe laughed. So did the other people watching.

"I guess they didn't bother to put the

snowman together too well when they got it here," Frank said to Joe.

"They had to do it in a hurry before anyone saw them," Joe said.

Danny pushed his way through the crowd. "I'm going to get even with you guys sometime. You'll see," he yelled as he ran away.

"I guess we'll have to make another head for our snowman," Frank said, looking at the pile of snow on the ground.

"Poor snowman," Joe said, picking up the buttons and carrot. "But it was worth it. Did you see Danny's face when the head fell on him?"

"And our snowman already won a blue ribbon," Frank said. "Maybe I should take Dad's lucky fishing hat home to him before Mom can send it to the thrift store."

"It *was* a lucky hat," Joe agreed. "It helped our snowman win a blue ribbon."

"And it helped us solve a mystery," Frank said.

Chet came over to join them. "Good

work, you guys," he said. "That was some pretty fancy detective work you did there."

Joe looked at Frank and smiled. "It was, wasn't it? We did just as Dad told us—follow the clues, and they'll lead you to the suspect. We followed the clues and we got them right!"

Frank nodded. "We sure did," he said. "You know what, Joe? The Clues Brothers are getting to be hot stuff!"

"You know what I think?" Chet asked.

"What?"

"You should use that certificate to the ice cream parlor before you lose it."

"Chet!" Joe laughed. "It's freezing cold today. How can you think of ice cream?"

"Easily," Chet said. "I'm always in the mood for ice cream."

"Okay, let's go," Frank said. "We can always have hot fudge topping to warm us up!"

BRAND-NEW SERIES!

Meet up with suspense and mystery in

FRANK AND JOE HARDY: THE CLUES BROTHERS™

▼

#1 The Gross Ghost Mystery

#2 The Karate Clue

#3 First Day, Worst Day

#4 Jump Shot Detectives

#5 Dinosaur Disaster

#6 Who Took the Book?

#7 The Abracadabra Case

#8 The Doggone Detectives

By Franklin W. Dixon

Look for a brand-new story every other month
at your local bookseller

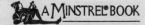 A MINSTREL® BOOK

Published by Pocket Books

1398-05

Do your younger brothers and sisters want to read books like yours?

Let them know there are books just for them!

THE NANCY DREW NOTEBOOKS ®

Look for a brand-new story every other month

Available from Minstrel® Books
Published by Pocket Books

1356-02

TAKE A RIDE
WITH THE KIDS ON BUS FIVE!

Natalie Adams and James Penny have just started
third grade. They like their teacher, and they like
Maple Street School. The only trouble is, they have
to ride bad old Bus Five to get there!

#1 THE BAD NEWS BULLY
Can Natalie and James stop the bully on Bus Five?

#2 WILD MAN AT THE WHEEL
When Mr. Balter calls in sick,
the kids get some strange new drivers.

#3 FINDERS KEEPERS
The kids on Bus Five keep losing things.
Is there a thief on board?

#4 I SURVIVED ON BUS FIVE
Bad luck turns into big fun
when Bus Five breaks down in a rainstorm.

BY MARCIA LEONARD
ILLUSTRATED BY JULIE DURRELL

 A MINSTREL® BOOK

Published by Pocket Books

1237-04